THE

PEANUT

For Erin, Isla, and JP Parrot

ALADDIN
An imprint of Simon & Schuster Children's Publishing Division
1230 Avenue of the Americas, New York, NY 10020
First Aladdin hardcover edition October 2013
Text and illustrations copyright © 2013 by Simon Rickerty
Originally published in Great Britain in 2013 by Simon & Schuster UK Ltd
All rights reserved, including the right of reproduction in whole or in part in any form.
ALADDIN is a trademark of Simon & Schuster, Inc., and related logo
is a registered trademark of Simon & Schuster, Inc.
For information about special discounts for bulk purchases, please contact
Simon & Schuster Special Sales at 1-866-506-1949 or business@simonandschuster.com.
The Simon & Schuster Speakers Bureau can bring authors to your live event.
For more information or to book an event contact the Simon & Schuster Speakers Bureau
at 1-866-248-3049 or visit our website at www.simonspeakers.com.
Manufactured in China 0713 SCP
2 4 6 8 10 9 7 5 3 1
Full CIP data for this book is available from the Library of Congress.
ISBN 978-1-4424-8364-4
ISBN 978-1-4424-8365-1 (eBook)

THE PEANUT

Simon Rickerty

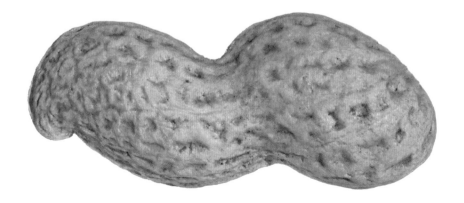

ALADDIN

London New York Toronto Sydney New Delhi

Eh?

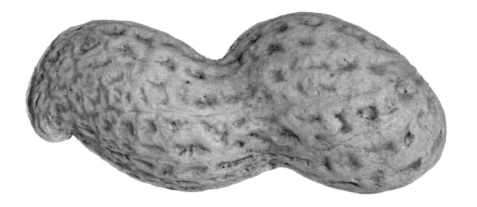

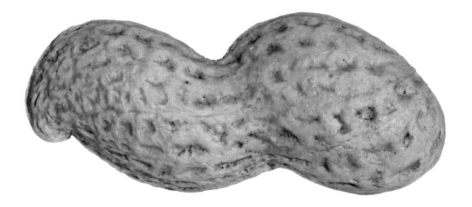

It's my chair.

No, it's *my* chair.

It's my hat.

It's my telephone.

It's my rattle.

It's my drum.

It's my boat.

It's my skateboard.

WHEEEEEEE

PING!

YUM!

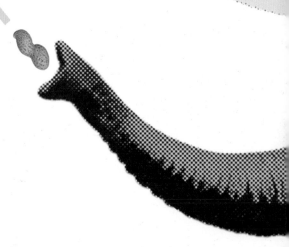

MUNCH,
MUNCH!

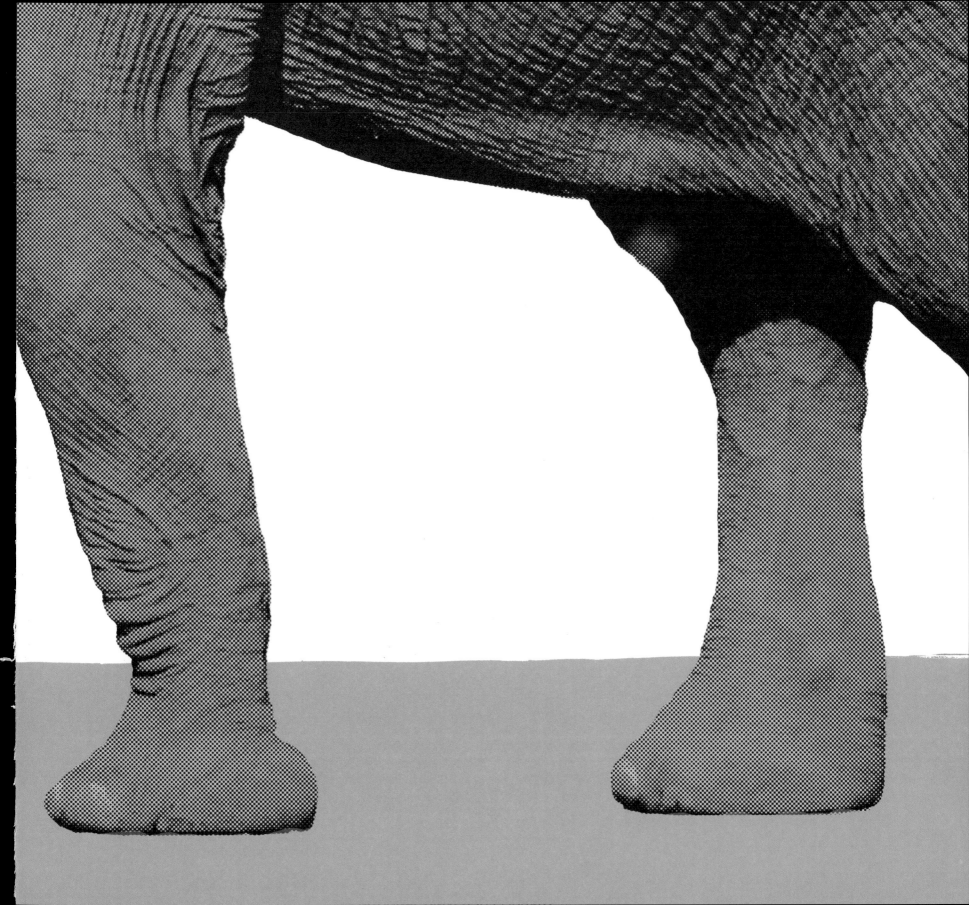

MINE!